ЗВЕНЯЩИЕ КЕДРЫ
РОССИИ

"Each citizen of Russia has the right to one hectare of his own land — is that not an outstanding national idea? Megre's books about Anastasia have served as a powerful motivator for national creation — is that not a miracle? And perhaps, at some point, a film about this amazing story will come out… I can say one thing for sure: Russia will be reborn starting in Siberia. There are still people left there who are capable of getting this challenging business off the ground. Time will show that I was right."

—**Aleksandr Mikhailov**, People's Artist of Russia

Yaak says that the series of books with the general title "Anastasia" powerfully influenced his decision to move out to the country. Yoala, who has mentally long been out in the country, exclaims: "This is a person who lives somewhere in the taiga. Vladimir Megre has written eight books about her. It would be beneficial for everyone to read them. Last summer I read them all one after the other and I thought, 'My God, what kind of life have I been living up until now!'"

—**Yaak Yoala**, Estonian singer

"Now, then, calculations have shown that V. Megre's achievement rating is R=5.3, i.e., his social significance is 200,000 times greater than the productivity of the average inhabitant of Earth. There are only a few such achievements per year in all areas.

Now I will announce that a rating of greater than 5 corresponds to the creative degree of 'Nationwide Academy Fellow of Public Development.' This is the highest degree from among those we've had occasion to confer. And we've also established a certain tolerance for pessimists, too!

Vladimir Nikolaevich, congratulations!"

—**Boris Alekseevich Minin**, President of
the International Public Development Academy

PARABLES

from chapters of the
RINGING CEDARS OF RUSSIA
book series

Russia,
First published in 2015

Author: *Vladimir Megre*
www.vmegre.com/en

Translation by: *Marian Schwartz and Susan Downing*

The PARABLES collection includes morality tales from chapters in the "Ringing Cedars of Russia" book series by Vladimir Megre. The parables that have gone into this collection have already become widely known, not only among the readers of Vladimir Megre's books in Russia and abroad, but also among people who haven't read this well-known series. Thanks to their subtlety, relevance, luminous imagery and deep philosophical meaning, they've done a good job of spreading via the Internet and have also been copied in print form, thereby gaining an ever-expanding audience of fans.

We seek the cooperation of translators and publishers.
For inquiries and suggestions please contact us at:
PO Box 44, 630121 Novosibirsk, Russia.
E-mail: ringingcedars@megre.ru
Phone: +7 (913) 383 0575
Skype: rc.press

Parables

Vladimir Megre

Parables

The
Ringing Cedars of Russia
Series

Russia, 2015

CONTENTS

A WIFE IS A GODDESS

From the book by Vladimir Megre "The Energy of Life" (translated by Marian Schwartz)

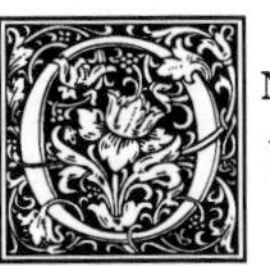 NCE UPON A TIME there lived in the world an ordinary husband and wife. The wife's name was Elena, the man's Ivan.

The husband would come home from work, sit in the armchair by the television, and read the paper. His wife, Elena, would cook dinner. She would serve her husband dinner and grumble that he did nothing useful around the house and made too little money. His wife's grumbling would irritate Ivan. He wouldn't say anything rude in reply, he would just think privately, "She's a sloppy hag herself, and she's making comments. When I just married, she was completely different, pretty and kind."

One day, when his grumbling wife asked Ivan to take out the garbage, he reluctantly tore himself away from the television and went into the courtyard. Returning, he stopped by the apartment house doors and prayed silently to God.

"My God, my God! What a muddled life mine's turned out to be. Am I really going to have to live my whole life with a wife like this? Grumbling and ugly to boot? This isn't life, it's nothing but torture."

Suddenly, Ivan heard the quiet voice of God.

"I could help you in your misfortune, My son. I could give you a beautiful goddess for a wife, but if your neighbors see a sudden change in your fate, they will be greatly mystified. Let's try this. I will gradually change your wife and instill in her the spirit of a goddess and improve her appearance. Only you must remember. If you want to live with a goddess, your life has to be worthy of a goddess."

"Thank you, God. Any guy would change his life for the sake of a goddess. Just tell me this. When will you start making changes with my wife?"

"I will change her a little right now, and every minute I will change her for the better."

Ivan walked into his apartment, sat down in his armchair, picked up the newspaper, and turned the television back on. Only he didn't feel like reading or watching a movie. He couldn't wait to look. Had his wife indeed changed just a little?

He stood up, opened the kitchen door, leaned against the doorjamb, and began to examine his wife closely. She was standing with her back to him, washing the dishes left after dinner.

Elena suddenly felt his gaze and turned toward the door. Their eyes met. Ivan examined his wife and thought, "No, no changes in my wife."

Seeing her husband's unusual attention and understanding nothing, Elena suddenly fixed her hair, and her cheeks flushed when she asked, "What is it, Ivan? Why are you looking at me so closely?"

Her husband couldn't think of what to say, and embarrassed himself, suddenly said, "Maybe I can help you wash the dishes? For some reason I thought. . . . "

"The dishes? Help me?" his amazed wife asked quietly, removing her soiled apron. "But I've already washed them."

"Well, that's great. She's changing right before my eyes," Ivan thought. "All of a sudden, she's prettier."

And he started drying the dishes.

The next day after work, Ivan hurried home impatiently. Oh, he couldn't wait to see his grumbling wife being gradually transformed into a goddess.

"What if there were suddenly a lot of the goddess in her, and I didn't change at all, like before? Just in case, I'll buy some flowers so I put my best foot forward."

The door opened, and a bewitched Ivan was lost for words. Elena stood before him in her party dress, the one he'd bought her the year before. She had a ribbon in her tidy hair. He became flustered and awkwardly handed her the flowers. He couldn't take his eyes off Elena.

She took the flowers and gasped slightly, lowering her eyelashes, and began to glow.

"Oh, how beautiful the goddess's eyelashes are! How meek her character! How unusual her inner beauty and outward appearance!"

Ivan gasped in turn when he saw the table set with their good service, two candles lit on the table, two wineglasses, and food drawing him with divine aromas.

When he sat down at the table, his wife Elena sat down across form him, too, but suddenly jumped up, saying, "Forgive me, I forgot to turn on the television for you. And here, I got fresh newspapers for you."

"I don't need the television, and I don't feel like reading the papers. It's always the same thing in them," Ivan replied sincerely. "Why don't you tell me how you'd like to spend your Saturday tomorrow?"

Completely stunned, Elena asked him, "What about you?"

"I had a chance to buy two theater tickets for us. But maybe in the afternoon you'd agree to go shopping. If we're going to be going to the theater, we should first stop by a store and buy a proper dress for you to go to the theater."

Ivan nearly blurted out the words "a proper dress for a goddess." He grew confused, looked at her, and gasped again. Sitting before him at the table was a goddess. Her face shone with happiness, and her eyes gleamed. Her intimate smile held a small question.

"Oh, my God, how beautiful goddesses are! And if she gets prettier every day, will I be able to be worthy of her?" Ivan thought, and a thought struck him like lightning. "I have to! I have to while my goddess is by my side. I have to ask her, and beg her to have my child. The child will be from me and the most beautiful goddess."

"What are you thinking about, Ivan? Is that excitement I see on your face?" Elena asked her husband.

He sat there agitated, not knowing how to utter his most cherished thought. It's no joke to ask a goddess for a child. God did not promise him a gift like that. Ivan didn't know how to express his wish, and he stood up, tugging the tablecloth, and said, turning red, "I don't know. . . . Maybe. . . . But I . . . wanted to say. . . . For a long time. . . . Yes, I want a child from you, beautiful goddess."

She, Elena, walked up to Ivan, her husband. From her love-filled eyes, a happy tear rolled down her rosy cheek. She put her hand on Ivan's shoulder and scorched him with her hot breath.

"Oh, it was night! Now it is morning! This is day! Oh, how beautiful life is with a goddess!" thought Ivan, as he put a coat on his second grandson to go for a walk.

TWO BROTHERS

From the book by Vladimir Megre "Co-creation" (translated by Marian Schwartz)

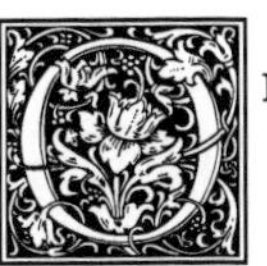NCE UPON A TIME—WHEN DOESN'T MATTER—there lived a man and wife. For a long time, they had no children. At an advanced age, the wife gave birth to two sons, two twins, two brothers. The births were difficult, and soon after she had borne the two sons, the woman departed for the other world.

The father hired a wet nurse and tried to rear his children. He raised them until the age of fourteen. But he himself died when the sons turned fifteen. The two brothers buried their father in sorrow and sat in their chamber—the two twins. Three minutes separated their appearance in the world, and so one was considered older and the other younger. After a mournful silence, the older brother spoke.

"As he was dying, our father expressed his sorrow to us that he had not had time to convey to us the wisdom of life. How will you and I live, my younger brother, without wisdom? Our line will continue unhappy without wisdom. Those who have had time to take wisdom from their fathers might laugh at us."

"Do not be sad," the younger told the older. "You are often in reverie. Perhaps time will see to it that you learn wisdom in your reverie. I will do everything you say. I can live without reverie, and living will be pleasant for me anyway. I rejoice when the day arrives and when the sun sets. I will simply live and work on the farm, and you will learn wisdom."

"Agreed," the older answered the younger. "Only wisdom cannot be sought by staying in the house. It is not here, no one has left it here,

no one will bring it to us here. But I have decided: I am the older brother, and I myself must find everything that is wise in the world for us both, for our line, which will live on down the ages. I must find it, bring it to our home, and give it to us and to our descendants. I will take everything of value our father left us and go all around the world, to all the wise men of different countries, learn all their sciences, and return to our dear home."

"Your journey will be long," the younger brother said compassionately. "We have a horse. Take the horse and wagon, load as much good as you can, so you will be less poor on the road. I will stay home and await the wiser you."

The brothers parted for a long time. Years passed. The older brother went from wise man to wise man, temple to temple, learned the teachings of the East and West, spent time in the North and in the South. He had a magnificent memory, and his sharp mind grasped quickly and remembered everything easily.

The older brother roamed the world for sixty years or so. His hair and beard turned gray. His keen mind kept wandering and learning wisdom, and he, now a gray wanderer, came to be considered the wisest of men. A throng of disciples followed him. He generously propagated his wisdom to their keen minds. Both young and old heeded him with delight. Great fame preceded him, informing settlements on his path of the wise man's great coming.

In his halo of glory, surrounded by a crowd of subservient disciples, the gray-haired wise man came closer and closer to the settlement where he was born and which he had left as a youth of fifteen, sixty years before.

All the people from the settlement came to meet him, and his younger brother, also with gray hair, ran out to greet him, rejoicing, and bowed his head before his brother, the wise man.

He joyously whispered, "Bless me, my brother and wise man. Come into our home, and I will wash your feet after your long journey. Come into our home, my wise brother, and rest."

With a majestic gesture, the wise man ordered all his pupils to remain on the hillock, accept the gifts of those who met them, and hold wise discussions. He followed his younger brother into the house. The majestic and gray-haired wise man sat down at the table in the chamber wearily. The younger brother began washing his feet with warm water and listening to the speeches of his brother and wise man.

"I have done my duty," the wise man told him. "I have learned the teachings of the great wise men and set forth my own teaching. I will not stay long in the house, for now teaching others is my lot. But since I promised to bring wisdom to our house, I will spend a day with you keeping this promise. In that time, I will tell you the wisest truths, my younger brother. Here is the first. All people must live in a beautiful garden."

Drying his feet with a clean, beautifully embroidered towel, the younger bustled about, trying to please the older, and he said to him, "Taste. On the table before you are fruits from our garden. I gathered the best of them for you."

The wise man ate all kinds of beautiful fruits thoughtfully and continued.

"It is essential that every person living on earth himself cultivate an ancestral tree. When he dies, that tree will remain as a good memory for his descendants. It will clean the air his descendants breathe. We must all breathe good air."

The younger brother rushed and bustled about and said. "Forgive me, my wise brother, I forgot to open the window so that you could breathe fresh air." He pulled back the curtain, opened the window, and continued. "Here, breathe the air of our two cedars. I planted them the year you left. I dug one hole for a sapling with my own shovel, and for the second hole I dug with the shovel you played with when we were children."

The wise man gazed thoughtfully at the trees and then continued.

"Love is a great emotion. Not everyone is given to live his life with love. There is a great wisdom: each person must strive for love every day."

"Oh, how wise you are, my older brother!" the younger exclaimed. "You have learned great wisdom, and I have lost my head before you. Forgive me, I have not even introduced you to my wife." And he shouted, turning toward the door: "Old woman, where are you, my helpmeet?"

"Here I am," a cheerful old woman appeared in the doorway carrying steaming pies on a platter. "I was held up with the pies."

She placed the pies on the table, and the cheerful old woman made a funny curtsey before the brothers. She walked up close to the younger, her spouse, and said in a half-whisper, but the older brother heard the whisper.

"And now, you men, forgive me, I am going now, I have to lie down."

"What's the matter with you, silly, all of a sudden deciding to rest? We have a dear guest, my own brother, while you . . ."

"It's not me, my head is spinning, and I feel a little nauseated."

"And why on earth would you be having any trouble here?"

"Maybe you are to blame. We must be having a child again," the old woman said with a laugh, running away.

"Forgive me, my brother," the younger brother apologized in embarrassment to the older. "She doesn't know the value of wisdom. She was always cheerful, and in her old age you see she remains a cheery sort."

The thoughtful wise man paused a little longer. The sound of children's voices interrupted his reverie. The wise man heard them and said, "Each person must strive to know great wisdom. How to raise children who are happy and just."

"Know, wise brother, I thirst to make my children and grandchildren happy. Here you see them coming in, my noisy grandkids."

Two boys no older than six and a little girl of about four were standing in the doorway arguing.

Trying to get them to settle down, the younger brother told them hurriedly, "Tell me quickly what has happened to you, you noisy children, and don't keep us from our conversation."

"Oh!" the smaller boy exclaimed. "One grandfather's turned into two. Which is ours and which isn't? How can we tell?"

"Here's our dear granddad, isn't it clear?"

And the little granddaughter ran up to the younger of the brothers, pressed her cheek to his leg, ruffled his beard, and prattled, "Granddad, dear granddad, I alone rushed to you to show you how I've learned to dance, and my brothers tagged along. One wants to draw with you. See? He brought his board and chalk. The second brought his pipe and horn, and he wants you to play the horn and pipe for him. But I decided to come see you first. Tell them all that. Send them back where they came from, Granddad."

"No, I came to draw first. Then my brother decided to come with me to play the horn," said the grandson with the thin piece of board.

"There are two of you granddads," the granddaughter prattled. "Will you decide which of us came first? Pick me or else I'll cry bitter tears."

The wise man looked at the grandchildren with a smile and sorrow. Preparing an answer and frowning as he concentrated, the wise man still did not say anything. The younger brother was bustling about and did not let the pause that arose lengthen.

He quickly took the horn from the child's hands and without thinking said, "There is no reason for you to argue at all. Dance, my beauty and hopper, and I will play a dance on the horn. My dear musician will help me play the pipe. And you, artist, draw what the sounds of the music draw and what the ballerina dances. Draw it. Now then, everyone get busy quickly."

The younger brother played a cheerful and beautiful melody on the pipe, and the grandchildren all repeated after him simultaneously,

choosing their favorite thing to depict. The future great musician tried not to lag behind on the melody on the pipe. As a ballerina, the little girl hopped, turning red, joyously depicting her dance. The future artist joyfully drew his picture.

The wise man was silent. The wise man learned. . . . When the merriment was over, he stood up and said, "Remember, my younger brother, our father's old chisel and hammer, give them to me. I want to chisel our main lesson in stone. I am leaving now. I probably will not return. Don't try to stop me, and don't wait."

The older brother left. The gray-haired wise man and his disciples walked up to the stone; the path went round that stone—the path that called the seeker of wisdom to distant lands away from his own home. The day passed, night came, and the gray-haired wise man hammered and chiseled an inscription in the stone. When the exhausted gray-haired old man finished, his disciples read the inscription on the stone:

"All you seek, wanderer, you carry with you. You will find nothing new, and you will lose with every step."

THE RICHEST GROOM

From the book by Vladimir Megre "The Family Book"
(translated by Marian Schwartz)

TWO NEIGHBORS LIVED IN a certain village. Their families were friendly, they worked to their delight on their own land. In the spring, the orchards bloomed on the two plots, and each contained a small woods. A son was born to each in the family. When the sons of the two friendly families grew up, one day the two families issued a firm decision at a holiday table: to put everything in their sons' hands.

"Let our sons now decide what to sow and when, and you and I, my friend, now must not contradict our sons with a look or a hint," one said.

"I agree," the other answered. "Let our sons, if they want, modify the house their own way. They themselves can choose their clothing and decide what livestock and goods they need."

"Fine," the other answered. "Let our sons be independent, and let them choose themselves worthy brides. We will find brides for our sons together, my friend."

Thus the two neighbors firmly decided. Their wives supported their initiative, and the families began to live under the control of their grown sons. However, from that time on, the lives of the two families began to differ.

In one, the son was energetic and took everyone into consideration. He began to be called first in the village. In the other, the son seemed pensive and sluggish, and people began to call him the second. The first cut and hauled off the young forest the father had planted to market. He bought a truck, to replace the horse, and a small tractor. The son of the first neighbor was considered enterprising. The entrepreneur determined that in the coming year the price of garlic was going to rise sharply. He wasn't wrong. He pulled out all the plantings from his land and sowed a field with garlic. Since they had given their word, the father and mother tried to help their son in everything. The family sold the garlic at a large profit. They began to build a huge house of modern materials with a hired crew. Still, the son-entrepreneur would not let up and calculated from morning until night what would be most profitable to plant in the field come spring. By winter's end he had determined that most profitable of all would be to sow the field in onions. Once again he sold his crop profitably, bought himself a car, and thought himself elegant.

One day, the sons of the two neighbors met on the road through the fields. One drove a car, the other a wagon harnessed to a frisky mare. The successful entrepreneur stopped his car, and a conversation took place between the two neighbors.

"Look, neighbor, I'm driving an elegant car, and you're still getting around in a cart. I'm building a big house, and you're living in your father's old one. Our fathers and mothers were always friends, and I too want to give you neighborly help. If you want, I'll suggest what's most profitable to sow your field with."

"Thank you for your desire to be helpful," the second neighbor answered from his cart, "but I treasure only freedom for my thoughts."

"Then I will not encroach upon the freedom of your thoughts. I only sincerely want to help you."

"Thank you for your sincerity, too, good neighbor. The inanimate—the car you're sitting in, for instance—takes away from freedom of thought."

"How can a car take that away? It can easily overtake your wagon, and while you're still riding to town, I can accomplish my business, all thanks to my car."

"Yes, your car can overtake my wagon, of course, but at the same time you are sitting behind the wheel and forced to hold on continuously, and you are constantly fiddling with switches as you go, looking at the instruments and the road the whole time. My horse goes slower than an automobile, but at the same time I don't have to do anything with it, so I'm not distracted from the movement of my thought. I can fall asleep and the horse will run home itself. You said you had problems with gasoline. The horse finds fodder in the pasture itself. Not only that, tell me where you're in such a hurry to get to in your car?"

"I want to buy spare parts in advance. I know what might break down in my car soon."

"So you mean you have learned so much about equipment that you can even picture all future breakdowns accurately?"

"Yes, I have! I studied equipment in special courses for three years. You remember, I invited you to attend the courses, too."

"You gave your thought over to this equipment for three years. Equipment that breaks down and gets old."

"Your horse will get old and die, too."

"Yes, of course, it will. But before that it will give birth to a foal. It will grow up, and I will ride it. The animate serves man forever, but the dead only cuts his time short."

"The whole village thinks your opinions strange. Everyone considers me successful and rich and you living merely at the expense of your aged father. You haven't even changed the look of the trees and bushes a tiny bit on your father's land."

"But I loved them. I tried to understand the purpose of all of them and the connections between them. I encouraged those starting to wither with my gaze and touch. Now everything will bloom this spring in accord, by itself, requiring no intervention, merely thirsting to offer up its fruits by summer and fall."

"Truly, my friend, you are an odd one." The entrepreneur sighed. "You are always walking around and admiring your homestead, your orchard and flowers. You say in this way that you are presenting your thoughts with freedom?"

"Yes."

"But why do you need free thought? What is the point of freedom of thought?"

"In order to know all the great creations. To be happier, to help you."

"Help me? You really have gone too far! I can take the best maiden in the village for my wife. Any of them would marry me. Everyone wants to be rich, to live in a spacious house and ride in my car."

"Being rich does not mean being happy."

"And being poor?"

"Being poor isn't good, either."

"Neither poor nor rich, then what?"

"Everyone needs enough. It is not bad to have a sufficiency as well, and an awareness of what is going on around you. After all, happiness does not come to people all of a sudden."

The entrepreneur grinned and drove away quickly. A year later, the two neighbor fathers met to consult. They decided it was time to find brides for their sons. When asked which of the village girls he would like to take for a wife, the son entrepreneur answered his father, "The daughter of the village elder is to my taste, and I want to take her for my wife."

"I see, my son, you have done wonderfully. The daughter of the village elder is the most beautiful in the entire district. Everyone who comes to visit our village from nearby villages and distant places goes into raptures when they see her. However, she is willful, you know. Even her parents cannot understand the mind of this unusual maiden. She could even be considered strange. Women from different villages have started coming to this young maiden more and more for advice and healing from their illnesses, and they are bringing their children as well."

"What of it, father? I am nobody's fool, either. In our village there is no home more spacious, no car better, than mine. In addition, I have twice seen her look at me long and hard."

The second father asked his son the same question.

"Who in the village is most to your liking, son?"

The youth replied, "I love the daughter of the village elder, father."

"What does she think of you, my son? Have you seen her loving gaze?"

"No, father. When I met her by chance, the maiden lowered her eyelashes."

The two neighbors decided to go together to propose marriage for their sons. They came and sat down in a dignified way.

The village elder called in his daughter and said to her, "Here, my daughter, matchmakers have come to see you, from two young men wishing to take you for a wife. We have come to a joint decision to let you determine which of the two is your chosen one. Can you tell us who he is right away or will you take until dawn to think it over?"

"I have spent quite a few dawns in dreams, Father," the young maiden said softly, "and I can give you an answer right away."

"Then speak, we are all waiting impatiently."

The beauty answered the matchmakers who had come as follows.

"Thank you, fathers, for your attention. Thank you to the matchmakers' sons for their desire to join their life to mine. You have raised handsome sons, fathers, and the choice as to which of the two to entrust my fate to might be difficult. But I want to bear children and I want my children to be happy. I want my children to live in plenty, in freedom and love, and so I have come to love the one who is richest of all."

The entrepreneur's father rose proudly. The second father sat with downcast eyes. But the maiden walked up to the second father, knelt before him, and said, without raising her eyelashes, "I want to live with your son."

The village elder rose from his seat as well. He wanted to see his daughter living in the house considered the finest in the village and so said sternly, "You have spoken correctly, my daughter. Your prudence has brought joy to a father's heart, but you did not approach and kneel to the richest in the village. The richest here is the other. Here he is."

The elder, pointing to the entrepreneur's father, added, "Their son has built a spacious house. They have a car, a tractor, and money."

The maiden moved closer to her father.

"Naturally, you are right, dear papa. But I was talking about children. What good will there be for children in the things you listed? The tractor will break down while they are growing up. The car will rust, and the house will fall into decay."

"That may be, but the children will have a lot of money, and they will acquire a new tractor, and car, and clothing."

"How much is 'a lot,' I wonder?"

The entrepreneur's father proudly smoothed his mustache and beard and answered gravely. "My son has so much money that if necessary he could immediately buy three farms like the one he already has. Furthermore, we can acquire not only two horses like the ones our neighbor has, but an entire herd."

Modestly lowering her eyelashes, the maiden replied, "I wish you and your son happiness, but there is not enough money on the whole Earth that could buy a father's garden, where each twig reaches out with love to the person who raised it. Money cannot buy the loyalty of a horse that played with your child as a foal. Your homestead will bring money. The homestead of my beloved will bring a sufficiency and love."

THE BEST PLACE IN HEAVEN

From the book by Vladimir Megre "The Family Book" (translated by Marian Schwartz)

OUR BROTHERS CAME TO a grave in order to honor the memory of their father, who had died many years before. The brothers wanted to find out whether their father abided in heaven or hell. They all came to the simultaneous desire that their father's soul appear before them and tell them how he was doing in the other world. Their father's image appeared before the brothers in a wondrous glow. The brothers were amazed and delighted, and when they came to their senses, they asked, "Tell us, Father, does your soul abide in heaven?"

"Yes, my sons," their father answered them, "my Soul delights in heaven."

"Tell us, Father," the brothers asked, "where will our souls end up after the death of our flesh?"

The father asked each of the brothers this question: "Tell me, my sons, how do you yourselves evaluate your earthly actions?"

The brothers answered their father in turn.

The oldest son said, "I became a great commander, father. I defended our native land from enemies, and no hostile foot entered it. I never oppressed the poor and weak. I tried to protect my soldiers, and I always honored God because I hope to get to heaven."

The second son answered his father: "I became a famous prophet. I preached to people about good and taught them to honor God. I reached great heights among those like me and high rank because I hope to get to heaven."

The third son answered his father: "I became a famous scholar. I have invented many devices to make human life easier. I have built many good structures for people. Always before setting to my task, I praise God and remember and honor His name, and so I hope to get to heaven."

The youngest brother answered his father: "Father, I am raising my orchard and laboring in my garden. I send vegetables and fruits from my beautiful garden to my brothers and try not to do anything bad, anything unpleasing to God, and so I hope to end up in heaven."

The father answered his sons: "Your souls, my sons, after your fleshly death, will abide in heaven."

The vision of their father vanished. The years passed, the brothers died, and their souls met in the heavenly garden, only their youngest brother's soul was not among them. Then the three brothers summoned their father, and when he appeared before them in his wondrous glow they asked, "Tell us, Father, why is the soul of your youngest brother not among us in the heavenly garden? A hundred years have passed in earthly calculation since we spoke with you at your grave."

"Do not worry, my sons, your youngest brother, too, abides in the heavenly garden. He is not by your side right now because your youngest brother at this moment is with God."

Another hundred years passed, and once again the brothers met in the heavenly garden, but once again their youngest brother was not among them. Again, the brothers summoned their father, and when he appeared they asked, "Now another hundred years have passed, but our youngest brother has not come to meet us, and no one has seen him in the heavenly garden. Tell us, father, where is our youngest brother?"

The father answered his three sons: "Your youngest brother is with God, and so he is not among you."

The brothers asked their father to show them where and how the youngest was with God. "Look," their father answered the brothers.

The brothers saw the Earth, and a most wondrous garden on it, which their youngest brother had cultivated during his lifetime. In the wondrous earthly garden, their youngest brother, looking younger, was explaining something to his child. His beauty of a wife was busy doing something nearby.

The brothers were amazed and asked their father, "Our youngest brother is still in his earthly garden, not in the heavenly one as we are. What is he guilty of before God? Why hasn't the flesh of our youngest brother died? More than a century has passed in earthly calculation, so why are we seeing him young? Has God changed the universal order?"

The father answered, "God has not changed the universal order, created from the beginning in great harmony and inspired love. Your brother's flesh has died more than once. But the best place for the soul is in the heavenly garden created by your own hands and heart. Just as for a loving mother and father, the child they create is always the most beautiful. Following the Divine order, the soul of your youngest brother should end up in the heavenly garden, but since that garden is on Earth, then it is reincarnated immediately in a new body in the earthly garden dear to it."

"Tell us, Father," the brothers continued. "You told us that our youngest brother is with God, but we do not see God near him in his garden."

The father told his three sons, "Your youngest brother, my sons, is tending to God's creations, the trees and grass. They are the Creator's materialized thoughts. By touching them with love and awareness, your youngest brother is thereby with God."

"Tell us, our father, will we ever return to Earth in fleshly guise?" the sons asked their father and heard in answer: "Your souls, my sons, now abide in the heavenly garden, and they can acquire earthly guise only in the event that someone creates a garden on earth for your souls that resembles the heavenly garden."

The brothers exclaimed, "Gardens are not created with love for someone else's soul. We ourselves, if we acquire flesh, will raise a heavenly garden on Earth."

But the father answered his sons: "That opportunity was already given to you, my sons."

He quietly began to move away. But once again the three brothers asked the father, "Our own dear father, show us your place in the heavenly garden. Why are you moving away from us?"

The father stopped and answered his three sons: "Look! There, next to your youngest brother in his garden, a spreading apple tree is blooming. Under the apple tree is a small cradle, and in it the beautiful little body of an infant has already moved its little hand. The infant's little body is beginning to wake up, and my soul lives in him. After all, I was the one who began raising this beautiful garden."

WHICH TEMPLE
SHALL GOD BE IN

**From the book by Vladimir Megre "The Family Book"
(translated by Marian Schwartz)**

THE PEOPLE IN ONE OF THE many settlements on Earth were living happily. There were ninety-nine families in this settlement. Each of the families had a beautiful house decorated with fanciful carving. The garden around the house bore fruit every year. It raised the vegetables and berries itself. People greeted the spring joyfully and took pleasure in the summer. The sequence of cheerful, friendly holidays gave birth to songs and dances. In winter, people rested from the daily rejoicing, and contemplating the heavens, they tried to decide whether the stars and moon could be woven into better patterns than they now had.

Once every three years, in July, these people gathered together in a glade at the edge of their settlement. Once every three years, God answered their questions in an ordinary voice. Invisible to the gaze of ordinary eyes, God was tangible to each and every person. Together with each resident of the settlement, he would decide how best to arrange life for the days to come. The conversation between the people and God was philosophical, but sometimes quite simple and jocular.

For example, a middle-aged man said to God, "What were you doing, God, at our holiday this summer, when we all gathered at dawn and you started soaking everyone with rain? The rain poured until dinnertime like a heavenly waterfall, and the sun began to shine only at dinnertime. What were you doing before dinnertime, sleeping?"

"Not sleeping," God replied. "Since dawn I had been thinking how best to act so that the holiday would come out wonderfully well. I saw how some of you, going to the holiday, were too lazy to wash with pure water. What should I do? They would spoil the holiday with their look. So I decided first to wash everyone and then scatter the clouds and let the sun's rays caress your bodies."

"Well, all right, if that's how it was," the man agreed, stealthily brushing a crumb of food from his whiskers and wiping the cherry stain from around his son's mouth.

"Tell me, God," a man, an elderly, thoughtful philosopher, asked God. "There are many stars above us in the sky. What does their fanciful pattern mean? Can I, if I choose a star that pleases my soul, when I grow weary of earthly life, settle there with my family?"

"The drawing of the heavenly bodies flickering in the dark tell us about the life of the entire Universe. A relaxed and collected soul will allow you to read the book of the sky. The book of the sky does not open up to idleness or mere curiosity but only to pure and significant intentions. And you can settle on a star. Each can choose a heavenly planet for himself. You must observe just one condition. You must become capable of creating better creations on the star you choose than on Earth."

A quite young girl jumped up from the grass, tossed her dark blond braid over her shoulder, raised her little face with its little snub nose, set her hands impudently on her hips, and suddenly told God, "I have a complaint for you, God. For two years I waited impatiently to express my complaint. Now I will. There is something wrong, something abnormal happening on Earth. All the people live like people, fall in love, get married, and make merry. So what am I guilty of? As soon as spring comes, freckles come out on my cheeks. There's nothing to wash them away with or color them. Did you think them up for your amusement, God? I'm demanding that in the new spring I not have a single freckle again."

"Oh, my daughter! There will be no freckles, no flecks on your beautiful little face in the spring. But I will call them what you want me to. If you consider freckles such an inconvenience for yourself, I will take them away next spring," God replied to the little girl.

But right then, at the other end of the glade, a well-built youth stood up, and with downcast eyes said quietly, addressing God, "We will have many things to accomplish in the spring. God, you will try to take part in each matter. Why should you waste your attention on freckles. Especially since they are so beautiful, I cannot imagine an image more beautiful than a young freckled girl."

"So what should I do?" God said thoughtfully. "The maiden asked, and I promised her."

"What do you mean, 'What should I do?'" the maiden intervened once again in the conversation. "The people say, 'you should busy yourself with more important matters than freckles.' But if we are talking about flecks, then I say you can add two, like this, for symmetry, here on my right cheek."

God smiled. This could be seen from the fact that the people smiled. Everyone knew that soon a new and beautiful family would be born in their settlement.

Thus the people lived with God in their amazing settlement. One day one hundred wise men came to see them. The joyful residents always greeted visitors with all kinds of food. The wise men tasted wonderful fruits and admired their unusual taste.

Then one of them said, "Oh, people, your life knows its measure and is beautiful. There is plenty and comfort in each house, but no culture in your communication with God. There is no glorification or worship of the Divinity."

"But why?" the alarmed residents attempted to object. "We communicate with God as we do to each other. We communicate once every three years. But every day He rises as the Sun. In the garden, He bustles around each house from spring on as the bee. In winter,

He covers the earth as snow. His affairs are clear to us, and we are glad each time."

"The way you have set this up is wrong," the wise men said. "We have come to teach you how to communicate with God. All over the world, palaces and temples have been built for him. In them, people can communicate with God every day, and we are going to teach you."

For three years, the residents of the settlement listened to the wise men. Each of the hundred defended his own theory as to how best to build a temple for God and what to do in the temple each day. Each of the wise men had his own theory. The residents of the settlement did not know which of the hundred wise teachings to choose. In addition, how were they to do this and not insult the wise men? So they decided, listening to them all, to build all the temples. One per family. But there were ninety-nine families in that village, and there were one hundred wise men. Hearing the decision of all the residents, the wise men became upset. This meant someone would not get a temple and someone would not receive offerings. They began to argue among themselves as to which of the theories for worshiping God was the most effective and to draw the settlement's residents into their debate. The debate heated up, and for the first time in many years the residents of the village forgot about their time for communicating with God. They did not gather in the glade as before on their appointed day.

Another three years passed. Around the settlement stood ninety-nine magnificent temples, and only the huts no longer shone like new. Some of the vegetables went unharvested, and worms began eating the fruits in the orchard.

"All this is because you do not have a complete faith," the wise men proclaimed in the different temples. "Bring more gifts to the temple, and worship God more diligently and more often."

Only one wise man, the one left without a temple, on the sly told one and then another, "You have done everything wrong, people. All the temples you have built are of the wrong construction, and you are

worshiping in the temples incorrectly, uttering the wrong words in your prayers. I alone can teach you how you can communicate with God every day."

As soon as he was able to convince someone, a new temple rose up, while one of the existing ones immediately fell into decay. Once again, the one wise man who was left without offerings secretly tried to defame the others before the people. Quite a few years passed. One day, the people remembered their former gatherings on the glade where they heard God's voice. Once again they gathered in the glade and began asking questions in the hope that God would hear them and answer as before.

"Answer us. Why has it happened that our orchards yield wormy fruits? Why don't vegetables grow in our gardens every year? Why do people quarrel among themselves, fight, and argue, but cannot choose the best faith for all? Tell us, in which of the temples built for you do you live?"

God did not answer their questions for a long time. When His voice was heard in the dimension, it was weary, not cheerful. God replied to those gathered, "My sons and my daughters. In your houses, surrounded by gardens, there is today desolation because there was too much for me to do alone. Everything was conceived of initially by the dream that only together with you could I create what was beautiful, but you turned away in part from your own garden and house. I cannot create alone, the creation must be joint. I also want to tell you all that love and the freedom of choice are in you yourselves, and I am prepared to follow your wishes with the dream. But you must answer me, my dear sons and daughters, which of the temples should I take up residence in? You are all equal before me, so where should I be so as not to hurt anyone? When you decide the question of which of the temples I should reside in, I will follow your collective will."

Thus God answered them all and then fell silent. The people of the settlement, which was once beautiful, have continued their debate to

this day. There is desolation and decay in their houses. Around them, the temples rise higher and higher, and the debate grows ever sharper.

DEMON CRACY

**From the book by Vladimir Megre
"The New Civilization", part I
(translated by Susan Downing)**

THE SLAVES WALKED SLOWLY, one after the other, and each bore a polished stone. Four columns of slaves, each one and a half kilometers in length, stretched from the stone polishers to the spot where the construction of the fort city had begun. Sentries guarded the columns, with one armed sentry soldier assigned to each ten slaves. At some distance from the walking slaves, on the summit of a thirteen-meter high, man-made mountain of polished stone, sat Cracy, one of the high priests; for four months now, he had been silently observing all that transpired. No one distracted him. No one dared interrupt his reflection with so much as a glance. The slaves and the guards perceived the man-made mountain with the throne at its summit as an integral feature of the landscape. And the person – now sitting motionless on the throne, now strolling across the open area at the summit – attracted no one's attention. Cracy had set himself a goal: he would reconstruct the government, fortify the priests' power for a millennium to come, bring all the people of the Earth under their control and turn all of them, including the rulers of governments, into slaves of the priests.

* * *

One day Cracy came down from the mountain, leaving his double behind him on the throne. The priest changed his clothing and removed his wig. Then he ordered the leader of the sentries to shackle him in chains like a simple slave and put him into the column behind a strong, young slave by the name of Nard.

Peering into the faces of the slaves, Cracy noticed that this young man's gaze was not wandering or distant like those of many others, but rather, inquisitive and calculating. Nard's face was at turns focused and thoughtful, or agitated. "That means he's conjuring up some kind of plan," the priest concluded, but he wanted to ascertain how accurate his observation might be.

For two days Cracy followed Nard, silently hauling stones, sitting next to him at meals and sleeping in the bunk next to his. On the third night, as soon as the command "Sleep" had been given, Cracy turned to the young slave, and in a whisper full of despair and bitterness, he uttered a question, addressed to no one in particular: "Will it really go on like this for the rest of our lives?"

The priest saw the young slave give a start and instantly turn his face toward the priest, his eyes shining. Even in the dim light of the barracks' lamps, they gleamed.

"It won't go on this way for long. I'm working out a plan. And you can be part of it, too, old man," the young slave whispered.

"What kind of plan?" the priest asked indifferently, sighing.

Nard began to explain, heatedly and confidently:

"You, old man, and I and all of us – before long we'll be free men instead of slaves. Count them up, old man: there's one sentry for each ten slaves. And there's only one sentry for the fifteen female slaves who do cooking and sewing. If we all attack the sentries at an appointed time, then we'll conquer them. Even though they're armed and we're shackled in chains. It's ten of us to one of them, and we can use the chains as weapons, too, and use them to defend ourselves from the blows of their swords. We'll disarm all the sentries, tie them up and take control of their weapons."

"Ah, young man," said Cracy, sighing once more, and then he apathetically replied:

"You haven't thought your plan through: it's possible to disarm the sentries guarding us, but the ruler will quickly send new ones, perhaps even an entire army, and they'll kill the rebellious slaves."

"I've thought about that, too, old man. We'll have to pick a time when the army won't be around. And that time is coming. We can all see they're readying the army for a campaign. They're gathering provisions for a three-month trip. That means that in three months, the army will arrive at its destination and engage in combat. It will be weakened by the battle, but it will emerge victorious and will seize a great number of new slaves. New barracks are already being built for them. We will need to begin disarming the sentries as soon as our ruler's army enters into battle with the other army. It will take messengers a month to deliver the message that they need to return immediately. It will take the weakened army no less than three months to return. In the space of these four months we'll be able to ready ourselves to meet them. There will be no fewer of us than there are soldiers in the army. When the captured slaves see what's happened, they'll want to side with us. I've planned everything out just right, old man."

The priest answered, now in an encouraging tone, "It's true, young man, with your plan and your thoughts, you can disarm the sentries and gain victory over the army." And then he added, "But what will the slaves do next, and what will happen to the rulers, the sentries and the soldiers?"

"I haven't given that much thought. One thing has occurred to me so far: all who were once slaves will be non-slaves. All who today are non-slaves will be slaves," Nard answered somewhat tentatively, as if thinking out loud.

"And what about the priests? Tell me, young one, once you attain victory, will you count the priests as slaves or non-slaves?"

"The priests? I haven't given that much thought, either. But what I would suggest at the moment is this: let the priests remain as they are. Slaves and rulers alike listen to them. They may be difficult to

understand at times, but I think they're harmless. Let them go ahead and tell us about the gods, but we ourselves know the best way to live our lives."

"The best way, that's good," the priest answered and pretended that he was terribly sleepy.

But Cracy did not sleep at all that night. He pondered. "Of course," thought Cracy, "the easiest thing to do would be to inform the ruler of this plot and seize the young slave. He's clearly the main source of inspiration for the others. But that wouldn't solve the problem. The slaves will always have the desire to be free from slavery. New leaders will appear, and new plans will be developed, and since that's the case, the main threat to the State will always come from inside the State."

A task lay before Cracy: to develop a plan for enslaving the entire world. He understood that it would be impossible to achieve this goal through physical force alone. He would need to exert psychological influence on each person, on entire peoples. He would need to transform people's thinking and instill in everyone the idea that slavery was, in fact, the greatest good. He'd need to set in motion a self-perpetuating program that would cause entire peoples to feel disoriented spatially, temporally and conceptually. But most importantly, disoriented in terms of their normal perception of reality. Cracy's thought worked faster and faster, and he no longer felt his body or the heavy shackles on his hands and feet. And suddenly, the program arose, like a flash of lightning. He didn't yet know the details, and he couldn't yet explain it, but he could already sense it, and it was astounding in its scale. Cracy felt like the absolute ruler of the world.

The priest lay on his bunk, shackled in irons, and he was delighted with himself: "Tomorrow morning when they lead us all out to work, I'll give a prearranged signal, and the head of security will see to it that I'm taken out of the column of slaves and that my shackles are removed. I will lay out the details of my program, utter but a few words, and the world will begin to change. Unbelievable! Just a few words – and the entire world will submit to me, to my thought. God really did give man a power that has no equal in the Universe – the power of human thought. It creates words and changes the course of history.

"An unusually fortuitous situation has come about. The slaves have readied a plan for rebellion. It's rational, this plan, and it's clear it could lead to a result that would be positive for them in the short run. But with just a few phrases, I will turn not just them – but the descendants of today's slaves too, and even all the earth's rulers, too – into slaves. I'll force them all to be slaves for thousands of years to come."

In the morning, when Cracy gave the signal, the head of security removed his shackles. And right away, the next day, he invited the remaining priests and the pharaoh to his observation platform. Cracy began his speech to those who had assembled:

"No one is to write down or pass on what you are about to hear. No walls surround us, and no one aside from you shall hear my words. I have conceived a way of turning all people living on the Earth into slaves of our pharaoh. This is something that is impossible to achieve even with the help of countless troops and exhausting wars. Yet I shall achieve it with but a few sentences. Once they have been pronounced, only two days will pass, and then you will see how the world will begin to change. Look: down below us, long columns of slaves shackled in chains are carrying one stone each. They're guarded by a multitude of soldiers. The more slaves there are, the better it is for the government. That's the way we have always seen it. But the more slaves there are, the more we end up fearing their rebellion. We increase security. We are forced to feed our slaves well, because otherwise they'll be unable to do this hard physical labor. Even so, they are lazy and inclined to rebellion. Look how slowly they move, but the sentry has grown lazy. He's not urging them on with the cat o' nine tails, and he's not beating even the strong and healthy slaves. But soon they'll be moving much faster. They will need no guards. The sentries, too, will become slaves. Here is how we can achieve this. Today at sunset, let the heralds issue

the pharaoh's decree, which will declare: "With the dawn of the new day, all slaves will be granted complete freedom. For each stone that he delivers to the city, each free man will receive one gold coin. The coins can be exchanged for food, clothing, shelter, a palace in the city, and for the city itself. From this day forward, you are free men."

When the priests grasped the full import of what Cracy had said, one of them, the oldest among them, uttered these words:

"You are a demon, Cracy. Your conception will enshroud a great number of the earth's peoples in demonism."

"So let it be said that I am a demon. And let it be, that in the future, people will call this conception of mine democracy."

* * *

At sunset the decree was issued to the slaves. They were astounded, and many were unable to sleep that night, as they contemplated their new and happy life.

The next morning the priests and the pharaoh once again ascended to the platform atop the man-made mountain. They could not have imagined the scene they now saw before them. Thousands of people, former slaves, were racing against each other to haul the very same stones as before. Many, the sweat streaming off them, were carrying two stones each. Others, carrying one stone, were running along, kicking up the dust. There were also several sentries hauling stones. These people, who now thought of themselves as free – after all, their chains had been removed – were striving to acquire as many of the coins they were lusting after as possible, so that they could build their happy lives.

Cracy spent a few more months on his platform, gazing with satisfaction at what was transpiring below. The changes were immense. Some of the slaves had united into small groups and constructed carts. After loading these carts to the top with stones, they'd push them along, streaming with sweat.

"They will invent still more devices," Cracy thought to himself with satisfaction. "Why, even now, people have begun providing domestic services: they deliver water and food. Some of the slaves

eat on the go, not wanting to spend time going back to the barracks to eat, and they pay those who bring them food out of the coins they earn. And look! Healers have appeared, too. They treat those who are ailing on the go, and they, too, receive coins. And they've chosen traffic controllers. Soon they'll choose bosses and judges for themselves. Fine, let them do that. After all, they consider themselves free, but what's at the core of it hasn't changed: they're still hauling stones…"

And they have been running this way through the millennia, in the dust, streaming with sweat, hauling stones. And even today these slaves' descendants continue their senseless running…

OHE CANDLE

From Vladimir Megre's appearance at the third annual International "Ringing Cedars" Festival (translated by Susan Downing)

GROUP OF PEOPLE was walking along. And they came to an abyss. They couldn't turn back—behind them was a raging torrent of water. Before them—an abyss. And an angel came down to them from Heaven and said: "I will save you. I will now turn into a hot air balloon with a basket. You can all get into it, and I will carry you across this abyss. All I ask of you is this: if my strength gives out, then each of you must light a candle or a lighter, in order to warm the air in the balloon, so it can continue its flight." The people got in, and each of them took one of these lighters. And the hot air balloon took flight. It still had a tiny distance to fly to cross the abyss, when the angel began losing strength, and he said: "Please, light the candle I gave you." And the people stood up and lit their candles. But one person remained sitting in the corner, just warming his hands with the lighted candle the angel had given him. The balloon needed the flame of but one more candle to be able to continue its flight and carry all the people away. And the balloon stayed where it was. Here's what happened when even just one person was unable to comprehend, unable to light the candle—the energy—given to him.

QUOTES

From the books by Vladimir Megre
of the "Ringing Cedars of Russia" series

The spiritual, the material—everything has to be sensed equally. Then life is stable, and you can stand on two feet.

—Anastasia's grandfather, "Co-creation"

All universal wisdom is contained in each human soul in perpetuity, from the moment of the soul's creation. Wise men often lead souls away from the main thing for their own benefit without further ado.

—Anastasia, "Co-creation"

For millions of years, there has existed a multitude of teachings. And all about one and the same thing, that mankind should live in expectation of receiving something from someone. And mankind has done so, closing off its thought and rationality. It has not thought about why and to what end the Universe lights up the stars above man.

—Anastasia's grandfather, "Anasta"

The significant books are those books which shape a given way of life of a segment of the human community.

—Anastasia's grandfather, "The Energy of Life"

All that exists has a connection with the entire Universe. The pinnacle of all creations is man... Man's purpose is to know everything around him and to create something beautiful in the Universe...

—Anastasia, "The Family Book"

Being rich does not mean being happy... Everyone needs enough. It is not bad to have a sufficiency as well, and an awareness of what is going on around you. After all, happiness does not come to people all of a sudden.

—Neighbor's son from the Anastasia's parable, "The Family Book"

Many religions of all times have spoken of God, but none of them talks about the obvious. By consciously communicating with nature, man is communicating with Divine thought. Understanding the dimension means understand God.

—Anastasia, "The Family Book"

...a person can be considered spiritual if he is capable of undertaking actions beneficial to the Earth, his family, and his parents, that is, to God. If someone who calls himself spiritual cannot make himself, the woman he loves, his family, and his children happy, then that is pseudo-spirituality.

—Vladimir Megre, "Who Are We?"

His words? There are so many words with different meanings among earthly nations. So many dissimilar languages and dialects. But there is one language for all, one language of Divine appeals for all. It is woven from the rustling of leaves, the singing of birds, and the waves. God's language has smells and color. God gives a prayerful answer in this language to each request and prayer.

—Anastasia, "Co-creation"

Consciousness will serve as the beginning of everything. The aspiration of thought will find the optimal route like a river. …Sincere feelings are in those who themselves erected this oasis of paradise, who embodied their soul's good amid the fuss and gloom of death.

—**Anastasia**, "The Dimension of Love"

For centuries seekers have been looking for a holy place on Earth. They believe it is called Shambala and that in that place a connection can happen between anyone and the universal wisdom. …And they will not find it if they keep searching this way, for Shambala is inside each of us, and its outward manifestation is recreated by people.

—**Anastasia**, "The Dimension of Love"

To the end of their days, most people are incapable of realizing the truth. You'd think it was a simple question: What is the meaning of life? Yet it remains unanswered. But the meaning of life lies in truth, joy, and love.

—**Anastasia**, "Anastasia"

Those who are able to understand their destiny and the essence of infinity will begin to live happily, reembodied eternally, for with their thoughts they themselves will create their own happy infinity.

—**Anastasia**, "Who Are We?"

An Appeal from Vladimir Megre to His Readers

Several Internet websites now share ideas that are very similar to those of the main character, Anastasia, in the "Ringing Cedars of Russia" series.

Many of these websites purport to be official and use the name "Vladimir Megre." They even answer letters in my name.

In this regard, I feel it is my duty to inform you, dear readers, of my decision to create an official international website:

www.vmegre.com/en

This will be the only official source for correspondence in all languages from my readers all over the world.

By registering at and subscribing to this website you will be eligible to receive information on the dates and locations of upcoming reader conferences, as well as other information.

Our unified website will keep you, dear readers, informed about the Ringing Cedars of Russia movement throughout the world.

Yours truly,
Vladimir Megre

THE
RINGING CEDARS OF RUSSIA
BOOK SERIES

*ARABLES* collection includes tales from several chapters from the "Ringing Cedars of Russia" book series which consists of 10 volumes. The author continues working on the next book.

The author holds readers' and press conferences in Russia and other countries.

The most active readers of the "Ringing Cedars of Russia" book series unite into public organizations, one of the aims of which is the creation of Kin's domains (homesteads). In 2010 another book *Anasta* was issued. The author plans to write a scenario on the basis of his books.

Throughout 1996-2006 nine books were written by Vladimir Megre (The *Ringing Cedars of Russia* Series: *Anastasia, Ringing Cedars of Russia, The Dimension of Love, Co-Creation, Who Are We?, The Family Book, The Energy of Life, The New Civilization, The New Civilization II: Rites of Love*). More than 11 million copies of the books translated into 20 languages have been sold worldwide. In 1999 Vladimir Megre established the Anastasia Foundation for the cultural support of Anastasia's philosophy and launched the site: www.Anastasia.ru.

BIOGRAPHY
OF THE AUTHOR
VLADIMIR MEGRE

V LADIMIR NIKOLAEVICH MEGRE (born 23 July, 1950 in Kuznichi village, Gorodnyansky District, Chernigov Region in Ukraine), the author of the "Ringing Cedars of Russia" book series, was a well-known entrepreneur. He spent most of his childhood with his grandmother Efrosinia Verkhusha, a village healer.

As a teenager Vladimir occasionally visited Father Feodorit, a priest of the *Trinity-Sergiyev Monastery*. Later he was shown there the picture "The One and Only" which he described in his second book before the picture was revealed to the world.

Vladimir started an independent life early and left the parents' house at the age of 16. Since 1974 he lived in Novosibirsk and worked as a photographer with *Novosibirskoblfoto*, a service company.

At the beginning of Perestroika (reforms of the late 1980s) he was the president of the Inter-Regional Association of Siberian Entrepreneurs. In 1994-5 he organized two large-scale trade expeditions with a fleet of river steamers along the River Ob along the route Novosibirsk – Salekhard – Novosibirsk at his own expense. On this trip, an encounter with Anastasia in the Siberian taiga changed his entire life.

It had been a secret for a long time for relatives and friends what made him, an entrepreneur with ten years experience, to pledge his property and spend his savings on unprofitable trading trips. The mys-

tery was revealed in his books with Anastasia as the main character. Vladimir Megre brought something really invaluable from the trips.

Throughout 1996-2006 nine books were written by Vladimir Megre (*The Ringing Cedars of Russia Series*: *Anastasia, The Ringing Cedars of Russia, The Space of Love, Co-Creation, Who Are We?, Book of Kin, The Energy of Life, The New Civilization, Rites of Love*).

In 2011 the author became Laureate of *Gusi Peace Prize.*

By now 11 millions copies of the books translated into 20 languages have been sold. In 1999 Megre established the Anastasia Foundation for Culture and Creative Support in the city of Vladimir and launched the site www.Anastasia.ru.

The author holds readers' and press conferences in Russia and other countries.

The most active readers of Ringing Cedars of Russia book series unite into public organizations, one of the aims of which is the creation of Kin's domains. In 2010 another book "Anasta" was issued. The author plans to write a scenario on the basis of his books.

Official site of the author: www.vmegre.com/en

The author: Vladimir Megre
Original language: Russian

Volume I *Anastasia*
Volume II *Ringing Cedars of Russia*
Volume III *The Dimension of Love*
Volume IV *Co-creation*
Volume V *Who Are We?*
Volume VI *The Family Book*
Volume VII *The Energy of Life*
Volume VIII (Part I) *The New Civilization*
Volume VIII (Part II) *The New Civilization II: Rites of Love*
Volume X *Anasta*

According to the author's idea, the IXth volume is being written by his readers. These are the *Family Books*, kin annals.

Russia,

First published in 2015

Copyright: © *Vladimir Megre*

Translation by: *Marian Schwartz and Susan Downing*

Twitter: www.twitter.com/vmegre
Facebook: www.facebook.com/vmegre
Youtube: www.youtube.com/vmegrecom
Pinterest: www.pinterest.com/vladimirmegre

The official site of the author: www.vmegre.com/en

Barnes & Noble:
www.barnesandnoble.com/c/vladimir-megre

Amazon:
www.amazon.com/Vladimir-Megre/e/B00CP3AVKO

Apple iTunes:
www.itunes.apple.com/us/artist/vladimir-megre/id716468509?mt=11

Kobo:
www.kobobooks.com/search/search.html?q=%22Vladimir+Megre%22

Goodreads:
www.goodreads.com/author/show/3262221.Vladimir_Megr_

Shelfari:
www.shelfari.com/authors/a2916115/Vladimir-Megre

Instagram:
www.instagram.com/ringing_cedars_of_russia

The "Ringing Cedars" company presents products, self-manufactured in the taiga as well as products of Kin's domains: www.megrellc.com

International Ringing Cedars Portal: www.anastasia.ru

We seek the cooperation of translators and publishers.

For inquiries and suggestions please contact us at:
PO Box 44, 630121 Novosibirsk, Russia.
E-mail: ringingcedars@megre.ru
Phone.: +7 (913) 383 0575
Skype: rc.press

27994052R00035

Made in the USA
San Bernardino, CA
20 December 2015